KNIGHT OWL

CHRISTOPHER DENISE

Christy Ottaviano Books

LITTLE, BROWN AND COMPANY

New York Boston

Since the day he hatched,
Owl had one wish.

To be a knight.

Every morning before he drifted off to sleep,
he imagined himself as a *real* knight.
He would be brave. He would be clever.
And he would have many friends.
It was just a dream. Until one day…

Knights began disappearing from the castle.

So Owl applied to Knight School.

And to everyone's surprise, he was accepted!

Owl was an excellent student.

But he had a tough
time with a sword.

Even the smallest shield
was a problem.

And he had a habit of nodding
off during the day.

Knight School was hard, but Owl worked and worked.

He graduated with honor, as all knights do.

Owl was assigned to the Knight Night Watch.
He was very good at his job.

The other knights usually fell asleep during the long Knight Night Watch, but Owl didn't mind. All alone on the castle wall, he finally felt like a *real* knight.

Until late one evening, it was very dark
and very, very quiet, when…

Owl heard a strange sound.

Whoosh!!!

It sounded like a huge bird flapping its wings.

"Whooooo," Owl called.

He heard the sound again.

Whoosh, whoosh.
Whoosh, whoosh.

"Whoo, whoo," he called.

WHOOSH!

"Who, who, who, *whooooooooooo!*" Owl called.

"Whooo, me?" said a deep voice.

"Who you?" asked Owl.

"I am a hungry dragon," said the dragon.

Owl was very afraid.

But because he was now a *real* knight and knights
are brave, he puffed out his feathers and said,
"I am Owl, and I am a knight of the Night Watch!"

"You don't look like a knight," said the dragon.
"You look like a midnight snack."

Owl's feathers trembled.

But because he was a *real* knight and knights are clever, he said, "You don't want me. I am too small, hardly even a mouthful."

"A mouthful is enough," snarled the dragon.

"I am all feathers and fluff," said Owl.
"A great dragon like you needs something
tastier and more filling!

"How about a pizza instead?"

It turned out that the dragon loved pizza.

They talked about how each of them had hatched from eggs, how much they liked the night, and how flying was hard to explain to someone who had never done it before.

They really had a lot in common.

The following week, not a single knight disappeared.
Or the week after that.

And every night, Owl patrolled the walls.

It was very dark and very, very quiet.
But Owl didn't mind, because he was brave,
he was clever...

And he had many friends.

For my family, who helped
hatch Owl and all of his
dreams over a pizza dinner.

ABOUT THIS BOOK

The illustrations for this book were done using Adobe Photoshop, a Wacom tablet, Procreate, and an iPad. This book was edited by Christy Ottaviano and designed by Angelie Yap. The production was supervised by Lillian Sun, and the production editor was Jen Graham. The text was set in Brioso Pro, and the display type is hand lettered.

Christy Ottaviano Books • Hachette Book Group • 1290 Avenue of the Americas, New York, NY 10104 • Visit us at LBYR.com • First Edition: March 2022 • Christy Ottaviano Books is an imprint of Little, Brown and Company. • The Christy Ottaviano Books name and logo are trademarks of Hachette Book Group, Inc. • The publisher is not responsible for websites (or their content) that are not owned by the publisher. • Library of Congress Cataloging-in-Publication Data • Names: Denise, Christopher, author. • Title: Knight Owl / Christopher Denise. • Description: First edition. | New York : Little, Brown and Company, 2022. | "Christy Ottaviano Books." | Audience: Ages 4–8. | Summary: After achieving his dream of becoming a knight, a small owl protects the castle from a hungry dragon. • Identifiers: LCCN 2021005465 | ISBN 9780316310628 (hardcover) • Subjects: CYAC: Knights and knighthood—Fiction. | Owls—Fiction. • Classification: LCC PZ7.D41496 Kn 2022 | DDC [E]—dc23 • LC record available at https://lccn.loc.gov/2021005465 • ISBN 978-0-316-31062-8 • Printed in the United States of America • PHX • 10 9 8 7 6